15.00

DISCARDED

J

THE CHRISTMAS SECRET

the
Christmas Secret

by

DAVID DELAMARE

GREEN TIGER PRESS
Published by Simon & Schuster

New York · London · Toronto · Sydney · Tokyo · Singapore

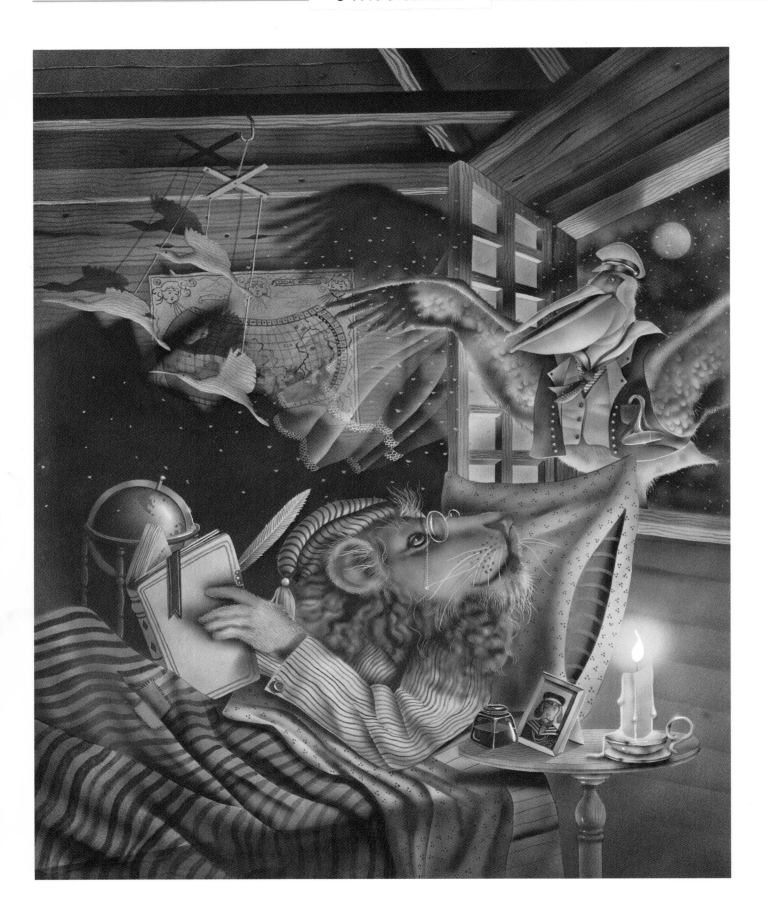

Richardson the lion was in bed, writing in his diary. At the top of the page, in his small, neat handwriting, he wrote: December the first, only twenty-four days to Christmas.

Outside in the cold night the wind howled, blowing flurries of snow against the window and rattling the windowpanes. It had been a hard winter. A sound came from the street below, the familiar jangle of the lamplighter's keys.

"Such a cold night for the poor lamplighter," thought Richardson, for he was a sympathetic sort, and then—for he was also a generous lion—"I think I'll give him one of my thick sweaters to keep him warm."

Suddenly, from outside, there was a tremendous whooshing noise, then the window burst open. Richardson whirled around and, for a moment, thought he must be dreaming. There on the windowledge, buffeted by the wind, stood a pelican, wearing a sea captain's hat. Richardson's eyes grew wide:

"Quilty? Quilty, is that you?"

The pelican heaved the window shut and said in a loud voice:

"Shiver me timbers, Chardy, it's a night to sink the lifeboats!" and he hopped sprily down from the window ledge.

"It *is* you!" cried Richardson, swinging his legs out of bed and rushing to greet his old navy captain. For a few moments they danced around together, slapping each other on the back and laughing. "But what on earth brings you here," asked the lion, "and on such a night?"

Quilty explained that he had been visiting his sister, Sara, who lived in a nearby village. "But listen, Chardy, there's worse to come of this weather. There's a storm brewing off the coast, worst I've ever seen, a regular blizzard. You'd better get all hatches battened down by Christmas. It's going to be rough." Richardson nodded solemnly. The captain was never wrong about the weather.

They warmed themselves in front of the fire for a while, then Quilty said:

"Here, my cub, I have something for you." He pulled an object from one of his pockets and handed it to Richardson. "For Christmas, let's say."

"Why, it's beautiful," said the surprised lion. In his hand lay a heavy glass sphere with a small brass ship inside it. "But, oh dear, I can't possibly accept this, when I have nothing to give you."

"Nothing to give me, eh?" interrupted Quilty. "Is that what you think?" He pointed to a battered leather accordion case in the corner. "And I suppose you've forgotten how to play that thing?"

As Richardson pulled the instrument from its case, it gave a faint, harmonious wheeze as though it had been shut up for a long time.

"What would you like to hear first?" asked Richardson. The tunes were already running through his head.

Quilty jumped to his feet: "The one we all sang after we scuppered those pirates off the Cape. What about that one?"

Richardson started to play and they both sang heartily.

There were many many tunes and a story to go with each one. Long into the night Quilty and Richardson sang and talked, and Quilty even danced a respectable hornpipe. But the wind was howling louder, and eventually Quilty had to take his leave.

"Don't forget what I told you about the storm," he said. "It'll be here before Christmas." And off he took into the night.

After the riproaring evening with Quilty, Richardson spent a restless night and awoke early the next morning feeling agitated. It was still dark.

As he lit the candles, Richardson thought about how quiet his life had become since he'd left the navy. "Too quiet," he thought wistfully, as he recalled the adventures he had had with Quilty at sea. Then he remembered what Quilty had said about the storm. "I wonder how long it will be before it gets here," said the lion to himself, "I wonder . . ." and he began to rummage through his navy trunk, looking for his navigating equipment.

He came across his old uniform, still neatly folded, and put it on. Then he took out telescope, charts, globe, books, even the brass sextant he had so carefully stored away, made himself a mug of tea, and sat down.

At first it was a slow process, but as he looked through the telescope and took measurements, it all started to come back to him. After a while the pages in his book were covered with calculations. He mulled over them.

It began to get light, and by now his tea was stone cold. Just a few more calculations . . .

After another hour he had it—the storm was due on Christmas Eve. He was sure of it! Richardson put down his pen and began absent-mindedly spinning the globe in front of him. "A storm on Christmas Eve," he thought, "most unfortunate for Santa, with all those toys to deliver." Richardson put his hand out to still the slowly-spinning globe and when his fingers fell on the North Pole, a most unpleasant thought occurred to him. What if the coming storm were so bad that Santa couldn't get through . . .

The building in which Richardson lived was owned by two pigs, Philo and Curdle, who also ran the Emporium on the ground floor. As Richardson finished putting away his charts and equipment upstairs, business in the Emporium was already under way as people came in to shop for Christmas gifts.

Philo was helping Mrs. Bruin-Brown, who wanted a hat for her husband.

"Show Mrs. B. that nice black one," said Curdle, helpfully, as his brother clambered up the ladder to the top shelf.

"Right," said Philo, reaching for the black top hat. As he came back down again he and Curdle exchanged a sly look and Philo said softly: "Good lad, Curdle, our most expensive one."

Philo and Curdle lived to make money, and the sound of the cash register was music to their ears.

Philo put on his most ingratiating smile and showed the hat to Mrs. B.

"Now, this is a fine hat, a very fine hat indeed," he began.

"How much?" demanded Mrs. B. She thought everything in the Emporium was overpriced, so she usually did her shopping in the next village, but that was three miles away and the foul weather had made the road treacherous.

Mr. Roland, a rabbit who had recently moved to the village with his large family, suddenly asked: "Aren't you getting any toys in for Christmas?"

Philo's eyes narrowed: "No toys," he replied in a gruff voice.

Curdle, who was the more cunning of the two, stepped in quickly. "Er, no room for them, you see," he said. "Can't stock everything," which wasn't the truth, but Mr. Roland wasn't to know that.

Years ago, when Richardson had first come to the village, the pigs asked him to make an entire range of toys for sale at the Emporium and Richardson had willingly agreed. Knowing how hard up the lion was, having just left the navy, the pigs paid him a pittance then sold the toys at an enormous profit. When word of this got to the attic mice—who had taken an immediate liking to the friendly lion—they were furious. One night they all crept into the Emporium and chewed up the pigs' money, right down to the last dollar bill. After that, the pigs never talked about toys again, and mice became their sworn enemies.

"No room to stock everything," said Curdle again. "What about a nice box of handkerchiefs instead?" But Mr. Roland had walked out in disgust.

Meanwhile Richardson was telling Tag about his concerns. Tag was a young descendant of the attic mice, a rather timid fellow who lived with his aunt.

"So you see, Tag, if it's a really bad storm, then Santa won't be able to get through. Can you imagine it? No toys for the children—think how miserable that would be."

Tag thought about the rocking horse he had asked for and said:

"Oh, terribly miserable. Awful. There's nothing to be done, though, is there? No way to stop the storm?"

"No, I'm afraid not," said Richardson. "Well, there is one thing. I could make toys for the children. If I only had the materials . . ."

"You could make wonderful toys," said Tag, and I could help you."

"But where am I going to get the materials?" said Richardson, "I'll need all kinds of things—wood, paint, glue. Where am I going to get the money to buy them?"

Richardson and Tag stared bleakly into space for several minutes. Then Richardson said: "There's only one thing for it. I'll have to sell some of my belongings."

"Sell your belongings?" said Tag, clearly impressed.

Richardson had made up his mind. "There's no other solution," he said. "But that still leaves one thing. . . and I don't know what we're going to do about it."

"What's that?" asked Tag, still eager to help.

"A Santa suit. I shall have to have a Santa suit."

Tag remembered the box he had discovered one night when he had been exploring the old stockrooms in the attic.

"I can get a Santa suit for you," he said.

"You can?" said the astonished lion. Tag told Richardson about his discovery.

"But won't it be missed?" asked Richardson.

"I don't think so," said Tag. "It's been there for such a long time, the box is covered with dust. Someone must have ordered it and not collected it."

"Well, that settles it," said Richardson, feeling more and more optimistic.

"Yes, that settles it," said Tag and he looked down at the floor so the lion wouldn't see the nervous look on his face. What Tag hadn't told Richardson was that the room in which he'd discovered the Santa suit was kept locked. He had crept in through a hole in the wall. The key to the room was on a chain with all the other keys to the building and Tag had no idea how he was going to get it, because Philo carried the chain in his pocket wherever he went. "I'll have to think of something," the mouse said to himself. "I've promised Richardson."

After Tag had left, Richardson looked around for what he could sell. There was his navigating equipment, but no one would want that, several books, a few ornaments, a picture frame or two, nothing that would fetch enough . . . then Richardson's eyes fell on his phonograph, his beloved phonograph.

"Philo and Curdle are always asking me if I want to sell it," he thought. "It's the only one in the village. I'll be able to name my own price. They won't make it easy for me though," thought Richardson nervously, "not those two."

So it was a nervous lion who carried the phonograph into the pigs' Emporium that afternoon. The two pigs tried to conceal their excitement, but there was no mistaking the greedy anticipation in their eyes, so Richardson drove the hardest bargain he dared, spurred on by his good cause.

Afterwards he went to the lumber yard, then the hardware store, and as he returned home through the snow, laden down with purchases, he thought: "Perhaps it won't be such a bad Christmas after all."

That very day Richardson set to work. He kept his eyes and ears open for what the children in the village wanted for Christmas so that he would know exactly what to make. One of Mrs. Chattermonkey's sons, Bobby, wanted a puppet theater and Richardson made a particularly fine job of that.

When Richardson asked Tag what he wanted for Christmas, the little mouse just looked distracted and said: "Oh, nothing, nothing." All Tag could think of was getting the key from Philo's key chain so that Richardson could have the Santa suit. He had decided it would have to be done at night, when the pigs were asleep, and just thinking about it made him tremble all over.

So Christmas drew nearer, the weather got worse and worse, and little Tag prepared himself for something more daring and dangerous than he had ever done in his life.

Philo and Curdle were getting ready for bed. Tomorrow was Christmas Day and they were looking forward to lying around, doing nothing except eating and drinking.

"I suppose there'll be another of those noisy get-togethers tomorrow," grumbled Philo, as he pulled back the covers on his bed.

"It seems not," replied Curdle. "I overheard Godfrey saying that he'd decided not to have one this year"—Godfrey was a cat who played the violin and usually threw a big party on Christmas Day for the whole village— "because Santa isn't coming."

"Stuff and nonsense," said Philo, yawning and hugging his piggy bank to his chest.

"Are all the traps down?" asked Curdle.

"All down," said Philo, very sleepily.

"Good. Well, goodnight," said Curdle, but Philo was already asleep.

Every night since the incident with the attic mice, the pigs had set a dozen traps on the floor of their bedroom, where they slept with their money. Tag's aunt never tired of telling him hair-raising stories of what happened to the mice that got caught in these traps. Although Tag loved to explore the Emporium at night, he had never ventured near the pigs' quarters. Until now . . .

From a tiny hole in the ceiling Tag could see the traps all over the floor of the pigs' bedroom. There was the sound of snoring. Philo's clothes lay on a chair with the key chain beside them. As Tag lowered himself down a length of string, Philo turned over in his sleep, so that if he were to open his eyes he would be looking straight at Tag! The little mouse shook with fear as he removed the key from the chain. It was almost as big as he was, and it made a noise when he took it off the chain. Philo snorted and seemed to wake up. Tag ducked behind the arm of the chair, wondering if he would ever see his aunt or Richardson or anyone in the world ever again.

Richardson was beginning to get anxious. It was ten o'clock on Christmas Eve and Tag hadn't appeared with the Santa suit. He watched the minutes tick by, ten-fifteen, ten-twenty—where on earth could Tag be? Then he heard a bump, which seemed to come from above, then another bump, then a whole set of bumps—BUMP BUMP BUMP BUMP BUMP BUMP BUMP—like someone falling downstairs. Richardson rushed to the door and looked out. At the bottom of the attic stairs was a large box lying on its side. At the top of the stairs was a very excited and out-of-breath Tag.

"I gave it a good push and down it went," cried Tag.

Richardson picked up the box: "Is this the suit?"

"Yes," answered Tag, coming down the stairs. "It must be a big one; that box was heavy."

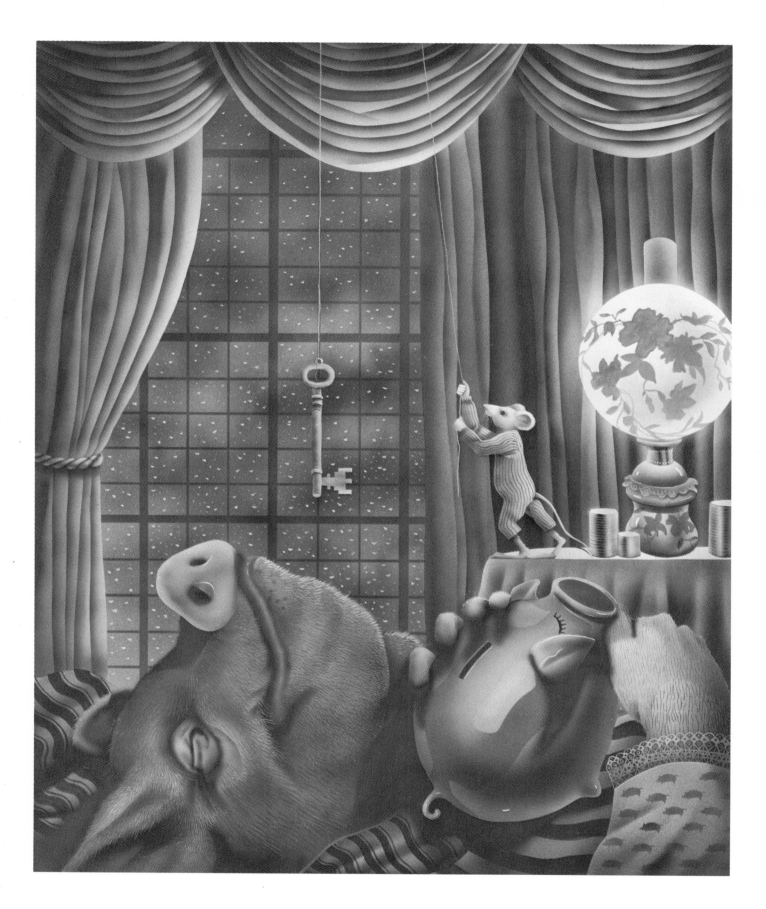

It was a very big suit indeed, and Richardson had to wear two thick sweaters underneath before it would fit. He pulled the furlined cap down on his head.

"How do I look?" he asked.

"Like Santa," squealed the delighted mouse, "just like Santa!"

At last Richardson hauled the sack of toys over his shoulder. "Well, here goes," he said. Then he looked at Tag with a serious expression on his face, put a finger to his lips and said: "Not a word about this, Tag. No one will ever know that Santa didn't come."

"I won't breathe a word," said Tag. "Richardson?" he said, as the lion opened the door to leave.

"What is it?"

"This is the finest thing I ever saw anybody do," said Tag. Then he added, "Good luck."

Tag went to the window and looked down as Richardson went out into the cold night. As the lion rounded the first corner, he was buffeted so hard by the blizzard that he could scarcely put one foot in front of the other. But he struggled on and somehow, many hours later, he had managed to deliver all the toys. Lowering his head against the driving snow he started to trudge home. He thought of his nice, warm, cozy, comfortable bed and an immense tiredness overcame him. "I don't think I've ever been so tired . . ." thought Richardson and, for a moment, it was as though he were already tucked in bed and the snowstorm was a dream.

As the dawn came up on Christmas morning, Bobby Chattermonkey awoke, leapt out of bed and drew back the curtains. Everything was white with snow, but the worst of the blizzard had blown over. Had Santa come?

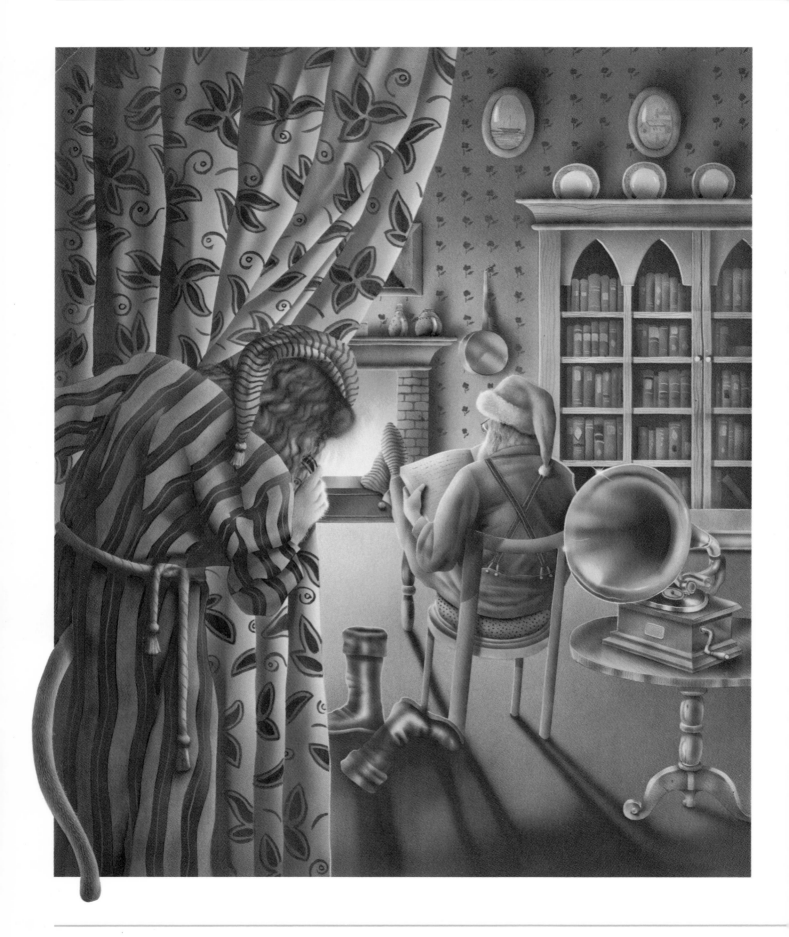

Richardson woke much later that morning and thought: "I haven't had such a good night's sleep since I was in the navy." He could hear music—probably the pigs trying out the phonograph.

Richardson took his robe off the peg behind the door and put it on.

"My robe feels a bit different today," he thought, sleepily. "That door looks a bit different, too." He looked around the room and realized IT WASN'T HIS ROOM!!!! Richardson was not one to panic. He seemed to hear Quilty's voice saying: "Stand fast, Chardy, my cub, then proceed with caution!"

Quietly and carefully, Richardson opened the door and followed the sound of the music. When he drew back a heavy curtain—there, in front of a blazing fire, toasting his toes and reading, sat a very familiar figure. Richardson stared in disbelief.

"Welcome to the North Pole and to my humble abode," said Santa Claus. "Here, come and sit by the fire, old chap. Sleep well?"

Richardson sat down, speechless.

"Quite a blizzard, wasn't it?" Santa continued. "Every few years it happens. The weather gets so bad that I can't get around or else I don't have all the toys ready in time. I really need a good man to help me. Of course, it's entirely up to you. Oh yes, but I thought you might like to see the place first.

"You brought me here?" asked Richardson, when he had recovered sufficiently to speak. Santa nodded. "So you did come to the village after all?"

Santa looked embarrassed: "Well, I, er . . . I was a little off course, in fact. I was supposed to be in the next village but, well, what with the snow and everything. You see my navigating isn't what it used to be. So that's why I thought I'd ask you if you'd be interested in helping me?"

"You want *me* to help *you*?" asked the amazed lion.

"Why yes!" replied Santa, enthusiastically. "When I saw what a splendid job you'd done on those toys and knowing your background at sea—why you're exactly the man I've been looking for—a toymaker with navigating skills.

You'd live here with us, of course," added Santa. Richardson looked around the cozy room—at the big bookcase stuffed with books, the blazing fire, and at the phonograph. Santa saw him looking at it and said, with a twinkle in his eye:

"How about a little Mozart? He's your favorite, isn't he? And by the way, Mrs. Claus is preparing the Christmas dinner. You, er, you might just want to wait until you've eaten before you decide."

Godfrey the cat looked on happily as his six kittens played with their Christmas presents and said: "Why, we should have that party after all." So after he had wrapped them up warmly, Godfrey sent the older kittens around the village to let everyone know that, since Santa had made it, there would be a Christmas party after all, an extra-special one.

And what a party it was. There was a beautiful tree, cake for everyone, party hats, all kinds of good things. Godfrey played his violin and everyone danced. Horace, who lived on the farm at the edge of the village, was the last to arrive. When he came into the room and saw all the fun and festivity, he started to dance before he'd even taken off his coat!

Tag looked around for Richardson but couldn't see him anywhere. "I wonder where he is?" thought the mouse. "Richardson should be here celebrating, too. After all, he was the one who made it possible." It occurred to Tag that Richardson might be catching up on some sleep after his hard night's work. Little did he know that, at that very moment, back at the North Pole . . .

Richardson finished his second helping of plum pudding and said:

"There's just one thing. Tag will wonder what happened to me. None of this would have happened without him so I should like him to know."

"Of course," said Santa. "Why not write him a nice, long letter. I'll get my best reindeer to deliver it."

T ag read the long, neatly-written letter all the way through twice, then he read the last part again, one more time.

". . . and so you see, Tag," Richard had written, "I'll be helping Santa with the toymaking and navigating, the two things I enjoy most in the whole world. I can't believe my good luck. But I wanted to tell you that none of this would have happened without your help. Santa said he never would have spotted me in that snowstorm if I hadn't been wearing the Santa suit."

Tag smiled to himself when he read that bit; it was his favorite part of the whole letter. He read on: "and when I told him that you didn't even get a present this year he said we'd have to make a very special effort next year. So think about what you would like and try to be patient. And remember, when you hear sleighbells on Christmas night, you'll know we are close by, and if you look out of your window you may catch a glimpse of us. But no one else is to know anything about this, Tag; it'll be our secret."

Tag carefully folded up the letter and put it away, thinking over the events of the last few weeks. He realized that if anyone deserved such a rich reward it was his friend the lion, and he was happy for him. And although he was asked many times if he knew why Richardson had left the village so suddenly, Tag told no one what had really happened.

A year went by and it was Christmas again. Tag wanted to stay up and sit at the window watching for Santa's sleigh, but his aunt insisted he go to bed. Tag did as he was told and he lay in bed, trying very hard to stay awake, but his eyes started to close and eventually he fell fast asleep.

He was awakened by the sound of sleighbells and leapt out of bed as fast as he could. He ran to the window just in time to see a sleigh disappearing into the starry night sky. Tag couldn't quite make out who was in the sleigh, but he waved and waved until the sleigh was quite out of sight. Then he dashed into the other room to see his present.

The sleigh sailed up into the night sky with Santa holding tightly onto the reins. "I thought I saw a little face at that last window," said Santa, smiling.

"Yes, that was Tag," replied Richardson. "I think he saw us; he was waving." He tucked his telescope under his arm and said: "Do you think he'll like his present?"

"Like it?" said Santa. "It was one of the best pieces of workmanship I've ever seen. And it's exactly what he wants. How could he not like it?"

"Yes, of course," said Richardson, reassured. "Of course he'll like it. Especially when he looks at it closely."

When Tag saw the rocking horse he just stood and stared at it for a few minutes. Then he climbed onto its back and began to rock, gently, back and forth, back and forth, back and forth, then a little faster and a little faster, until he was riding the wooden horse as though he'd done it all his life.

After a while, he let the horse slow down and climbed off again. He went around to look at the horse's face. It looked back at him with a serious expression.

"I think I'll call you Lionheart," he said, stroking the beautiful smooth wood, "after a friend of mine. Why, what's this?"

Under the horse's chin, Tag felt what seemed to be an unfinished part of the wood. He bent down to look at it and found something carved there. It was an inscription in neat letters and it said: "To Tag from Richardson, for keeping the Christmas Secret."

FOR MY GRANDMOTHER, IDA DELAMARE

DAVID DELAMARE
was born in Leicester, England and now makes
his home in Portland, Oregon where he attended
Portland State University. A fine artist who exhibits
frequently, he has previously illustrated two other
books for young readers: *The Hawk's Tale* and *The
Steadfast Tin Soldier*. *The Christmas Secret*
is the first book Mr. Delamare has both
written and illustrated.

My thanks to Pearl Watkins for invaluable assistance in the writing of this book. D.D.

GREEN TIGER PRESS, Simon & Schuster Building, Rockefeller Center, 1230 Avenue of
the Americas, New York, New York 10020. Copyright © 1991 by David Delamare.
All rights reserved including the right of reproduction in whole or in part in any form.
GREEN TIGER PRESS is an imprint of Simon & Schuster. Designed by Kathleen Westray.
Manufactured in the United States of America. 10 9 8 7 6 5 4 3 2 1
Library of Congress Cataloging-in-Publication Data
Delamare, David. The Christmas secret / by David Delamare. p.   cm.
Summary: Even though it seems that Santa won't be able to come because
of bad weather, two friends resolve to make Christmas as grand as ever.
[1. Christmas—Fiction.   2. Friendship—Fiction.   3. Animals—Fiction.]   I. Title.
PZ7.D3717Ch ' 1991   [Fic]—dc20   91-12779   CIP   ISBN 0-671-74822-X